SPANKED FOR BAD BEHAVIOR

Hucow Milking Story

Leandra Camilli

CONTENTS

CHAPTER 1

I opened the door to his room and then I stepped inside it. My hands were shaking and my heart was tight, but I still wanted to do this. I was in Deimour College, the main educational center for hucows. My breasts were filled with milk, and I wanted to get milked.

That was why I was so nervous and annoyed right now. They all said that it was going to happen, that I was going to be milked, that they were going to empty my udders, and a bunch of other promises, but then I realized that it was all a lie.

So, I was going to do something I shouldn't be doing. This was his bedroom. It was quite funny that he'd left it unlocked, but I wasn't going to complain. It was the kind of bedroom that one would expect for a teacher here at Deimour College. There was nothing out of the ordinary here. There was a single bed by one of the walls, a dresser, a nightstand, and a mirror.

I walked over to the mirror. I didn't like admitting this, but the truth was that I didn't think I was beautiful. Some of the teachers here at the college always said I was stunning, but I didn't really believe them.

I had dark, long hair that cascaded down my face and over my shoulders, flowing down my back. My eyes were as dark as it was. My skin was as white as snow, and perhaps the thing that most stood out about me was my milky, filled breasts.

They were so big now that I could even see the veins and a couple of other things almost trying to burst out.

They ached so much, reminding me how much I wanted to get

milked by one of those milking machines. It was such a pity that it wasn't going to happen today, and I also didn't have much hope that that was going to change in the following days.

If there was something I began to understand and learn about Deimour College, it was that the teachers didn't really care about us. All they cared about was selling us, and to be honest, it was working out for them.

This was Stephen's bedroom.

Even though it didn't have much, and it really shouldn't, he was well-off. His bank account was filled with money, and that was putting it mildly. He was one of the most-respected teachers in the Academy, and that was precisely so because all the hucows kept thinking about him, kept wanting to fuck him, and even though that was all infuriating, I wasn't going to deny that it also didn't make me feel the same way.

What I wouldn't do to have him knock me up, his seed in my belly, and finally nurture his baby.

That thought alone broke me out of my reverie after noticing that my lips were getting redder right in front of me in the reflection in the mirror. For a moment, I thought I was hallucinating, but it was really true. What they said about the effects of becoming a hucow was true, and I was seeing it all with my own eyes.

It was like I was becoming even younger than I was. I was 21. I now looked more like I was 19, which was something that made me feel slightly terrified. I didn't think that becoming a hucow could be so good for me in the long term. I mean, I had thought that coming here was the right call, but at the time, I still had my reservations, but now I realized that they were also pointless.

I turned around slowly, going to his dresser.

I opened the top drawer, finding what I was looking for. It was one of his underwear pieces. One of his boxer briefs, and it was white, and it was also slightly dirty. I could tell that he had washed it, but also that it hadn't been a thorough and deep wash, and thus I could see some marks and stains on the material.

For a lot of people, that would be a turnoff, but not for me.

I had come here exactly for this purpose. I wanted to see his manliness, feel it, smell it, and I was pretty certain that there was still some of that on his underwear.

Without giving it a second thought, I picked it up in my hand, and then I brought it closer to my nose. I smelled it. I sniffed it, and it was great. There wasn't enough of it – at least, not enough for me – but there was enough to allow me to make out his musky scent. That thing that was part of everything that made him the man he was, and after smelling that, my eyes almost rolled inside my head.

My fingers felt the material, pressing here and there, grazing on it, and I knew that it looked stupid, but I could also not stop what was already happening.

I knew that anyone looking at me now would think 'what the hell is wrong with her?' And they would be right to think that way.

I was still holding the boxer briefs in my hand when I realized that there was someone behind me. For a moment, I just noticed that I had forgotten to close the door to the bedroom. It could be anyone. I could see his shadow in front of me, and it was absolutely terrifying. I could feel how much my hands were shaking just thinking about what he was going to do now that he knew I was committing a 'crime.'

Well, perhaps not a crime, but certainly something that I shouldn't be seen doing. He was going to punish me, wasn't he?

He stepped inside the room, closing the door behind him, and then suddenly everything was dark. He started to step toward me, and I found myself frozen in place.

What was he going to do? I didn't know, but I didn't even like to think about it, especially because now I could already feel his hands working my shoulders.

"This is bad. This is bad, bad behavior, and you need to be punished for it, you understand?" He asked, his voice so close to my ear, and I could feel goosebumps on my skin, making the hair on it stand up. His fingers were rough, calloused, and he knew what he was doing, massaging my skin, pressing on all the right spots, and I knew that it was all over for me.

It was Stephen, and he had come for me. He had come here to punish me, and I could even feel his hard-on pressing against my butt.

CHAPTER 2

"**D**addy, what are you doing?" I asked, moving my hands up and then cupping my breasts. I was hoping that by doing that I was showing him exactly what I wanted. I wanted him to milk me, to wrap his lips around my nipples, or at least to put me in the milk machine, or something like that.

But what he was doing, his fingers working my shoulders, massaging them, was good enough, and I could feel wetness seeping out of my pussy. I was naked, like everybody here minus the teachers were, and it made all of this even more tempting and lust-inducing.

"I'm going to punish you, Denise. I told you that you weren't allowed to come inside my room, and you just decided to sneak in and not tell anyone about it. Not even your best friend, Ann, knows anything about this. I know that because I asked her about this. There's an alarm in my bedroom and it went off the moment you stepped inside."

"I'm so sorry. It's just that I really want this," I confessed, turning around and smiling. My smile was devilish. If he was thinking that he was already stilling fear in my heart, making me think less of the person I was, imagining that he had me under his full control, then he was soon going to find out that that wasn't exactly the case. I was stronger than this, and I knew that this presented the right opportunity to do something extremely naughty. I wanted the punishment that he was going to inflict on me.

And having said that, I showed him my udders. That was what

they were called. Udders. They were big, swollen, filled with my milk, and my nipples were harder than they had ever been.

Milk was even leaking out of them, and even though I couldn't see much of his face, I noticed his Adam's apple bobbing up and down. He really was turned on by what he was seeing, wasn't he?

I knew he was, but I still needed confirmation, and I was going to get that by putting my fingers under his pair of pants. He was dressed, just like all the other teachers, and it was disappointing. All these layers were only getting in the way.

"You are sorry?" He asked. "You think that something like that is going to make me forgive you for trespassing?"

"I'm hoping that you are going to realize that there's something much more important than this that you should be doing."

"And what would that be?" He asked, his voice so hot, so breathless, so deep, and in the meantime, all I could think about was how much I wanted him to kiss me. It was such a pity that Stephen would never do that. If there was something that all the other hucows told me about him, it was that he never kissed.

"Milk me. Empty my breasts. Drink, chug, and swallow all of my milk, and show me how much you want this. Show me how much you want me."

"Ohhh, I think I'm going to do a lot more than that," he purred, slipping his fingers under his shirt, lifting it, and the moment that he chucked it over his head, I was already with my hands all over his muscles, feeling the curves, the lines, the sweat on his skin, and pretty much every part of his torso. Stephen was much taller than me, and now that was even more noticeable than it had ever been.

"Then, what are you waiting for?" I asked, and even though I couldn't see much of his face, thanks to how dark it was, I knew he was smiling and his voice was as wicked as it had ever been.

He grabbed me, his hands around my arms, and then he took me to the bed. I thought he was going to make me lie down on it, but he had other plans in his mind. He sat down on it and then he put me on his lap. The first thing I noticed was his hard, massive cock pressing up against my belly, and I just wanted to reach down with my hand and start to stroke it. It was such a pity that I couldn't. It was physically impossible for me.

My bare butt was exposed to the delight of his eyes. Even though he couldn't see much, I knew he could still see my ass - and more than enough of it, of course. His hand roamed over my buttcheeks, feeling all the curves, and then he even slipped a finger along my butt crack.

The way he did that sent shivers of pleasure all through my body, and I thought I was going to come then and there. That was how much I was turned on right now, and I knew he was using that knowledge to his advantage.

"I'm going to spank you right now, Denise, and when I'm done with you, I doubt you will even be able to walk."

I couldn't believe that he was really going to spank me. My milk was still coming out and it stained his pants, but he didn't care about that. I knew Stephen was going to drag this out as much as he could. He would only milk me when he felt like it and now wasn't the moment for that.

It was the moment for something else. For when he finally brought down, with all of his strength, his hand on my butt, slapping it as many times as he wanted, punishing me until my ass was so sore that sitting anywhere would be difficult, if not impossible.

And even though it was going to hurt a lot, I knew that the punishment was well-deserved. Perhaps the thing about this that most stood out to me was that he had let me keep the pair of boxer briefs that I was still holding in my hands.

It was going to happen. He was going to smack my butt for the first time, and I could already feel tingles all over my skin.

CHAPTER 3

"You realize you deserve this, right?" He asked and all I could do was nod. Of course I knew I deserved the punishment and he was going to give me exactly that. Stephen held nothing back as he lifted his hand. This was all happening so slowly, and it was infuriating. He was dragging it out so much.

"I do," I said, and just when I thought he was going to smack my butt, he decided to do something else. He grabbed the pair of boxer briefs I was holding in my hand, bunched it up, and then put it into my mouth.

I looked up, trying to understand why he did that, and then he said, "I did that so that you don't scream much when I finally start to spank you."

Ahhh, so that was why he did it," I thought, turning my head so that I was looking down at the floor. I couldn't see much of it, the coldness of the stones seeping into my bare feet, making me wonder how I could even walk around here without complaining all the time.

Well, I wasn't thinking about that much, especially because I already felt the first smack on my butt, and it stung a lot. It sent shivers and waves of pain all through my body, and my back arched. I knew it was going to be painful, but I never thought it was going to feel like he'd just hit me with a heavy spoon or something even worse.

His hand massaged my butt, focusing on the part where he had hit me. There was a moment of silence, and I could hear his breathing.

"That was only the first smack. There's going to be more. About 20 for your infraction. Do you think that you can survive this? Do you think you can get through this without passing out?" He asked, his finger slipping inside my ass crack, and I thought he was going to look for my asshole, but he didn't. Stephen was always such a tease.

I couldn't even reply. His underwear, the thing that I had come here looking for, was in my mouth. It was a turn-on that it was in there and I could feel the smell coming from it stronger than before. It really was making it impossible for me to say anything right now.

All I could do was nod, which I did. That appeared to be enough for Stephen, I noticed, feeling his hand coming back down on my ass with enough force to leave a welt. And now I was feeling so much pain I was certain that I wouldn't be able to sit down anywhere without my body feeling even more pain than it was already feeling.

I couldn't hold back the tears. I was crying, and I couldn't do anything about that. And yet, I wasn't going to stop this. It was my punishment, and I deserved it. I deserved it because I thought I was being smart when I sneaked into his room, looking for his underwear.

At least now, I was holding it in my mouth and I could taste a part of him that he didn't want me to taste at all. After all, this underwear piece had been in direct contact with his prick, which was now pressing up against my belly. I knew that that was also part of his plan. Stephen wanted me to know how much I wanted his dick, to feel it inside of me, and it was all working.

In the meantime, milk was coming out of my udders, pooling on the floor, staining it, and I couldn't see much other than that. It kept on making me wonder when he would finally take me off his lap and then get down on his knees, lapping up all of my milk.

My back arched one more time.

He smacked my butt again with his hand.

Then, one more time and I felt my body shaking.

This was taking a huge toll on me, and I couldn't stop it anymore. It was happening, and with each passing second, I felt his hand hitting, smacking my butt, and it was a lot more than I thought I could take. Even breathing was becoming more difficult, and my entire body was getting sweaty.

Minutes later, I noticed that my wetness was seeping out of my pussy, and the volume that was coming out was increasing as time passed. That wasn't stopping Stephen from continuing the punishment, though.

And nothing could stop him, anyway.

After a couple more minutes, I felt like the punishment was going to go on forever, but then it stopped. His hands rested on my butt, massaging it, and I could feel his fingers moving over the welts.

"That was quite harsh for a punishment, don't you think?" He asked, and I couldn't even nod. I couldn't even do that because I was tired, sweating a lot, and huffing. I felt like I had just finished running a marathon, and that was putting it mildly.

And I also noticed that my milk was still leaking out of my nipples. When would I finally get milked? I didn't know, but I knew that I was on the verge of having an orgasm. One more thing he did, another push, and it would all be over.

And I knew he knew that, for he quickly slipped his finger into my anus, and then he started to rub it, spinning inside of it, and his pace was slow in the beginning before he picked it up.

It was absolutely exhilarating, and I couldn't stop myself when my body started to convulse. I finally came. I finally hit my orgasm, and it was as mouth watering as I'd thought.

And to think that there was still so much more to come... And especially now that someone had just opened the door, and I knew that it was another teacher.

He had come here for me as well.

CHAPTER 4

I knew his name. He was none other than Jason, and he was smoking hot. One of the hottest, most stunning, and most everything teachers in the college. His eyes were scrutinizing me, boring into me, and I couldn't help but wonder exactly what he was planning to do.

I felt more wetness coming out of my pussy, and then I noticed that Stephen let me off his lap. He let me fall down to the floor, and I was still sobbing and crying.

I still felt so much pain after the way that he punished me, and yet I also felt like I missed it already.

I felt his hand brushing my hair and my forehead, and I looked up and I found his intense, deep eyes looking at me. He was still smirking.

"You think this is over?" He asked, and looking down, I just noticed that his cock was finally out of his pants. Wait, when did that happen? I asked myself. One moment his cock was under his pants, something that annoyed me, and now it was finally out and it was pointing up.

"I never thought that," I replied. It was the only thing I could say.

Jason didn't bother with closing the door. He stepped inside the room, putting his fingers around his prick. He gave it a couple of strokes and then stepped toward me.

He was fast. One moment he was by the door, and now he was standing right in front of me. Where I was sitting, his dick was no more than a couple of inches from my mouth.

I could wrap my lips around his cockhead, and I couldn't wait until I was doing that, especially because he was leaking pre-cum from the tip. He was turned on, and I knew how much he wanted me.

Then, as if he gave me permission for that, he moved his hand away. I took a deep breath, put my hands on his legs, moving them up and down. Deep, thick fur covered his thighs, and I loved it.

"Take your time, sweetheart. We know how much you want this. We know much you've been thinking about this moment," he said, and I almost couldn't contain the excitement I felt in me. I felt it was going to burst out. I started to giggle, but then I stopped doing that.

My dream was becoming real. I was going to lose the virginity of my mouth with his dick, and I couldn't have asked for something better.

Kissing? Forget that. It wasn't for me. The only thing that I wanted from him was his massive prick filling one of my holes, and now that was finally happening.

When my lips were around his cockhead, the first thing I did was to start swirling my tongue on it, feeling all the curves, the texture, and everything else. I also felt his pre-cum on my tongue, and it was exhilarating.

After letting him feel what I was doing, the next thing he did was start to moan, his hand brushing my forehead, and then he bunched some of my hair in his hand.

He wanted to dictate the pace, and there was nothing I could do about that. I could focus only on what I was doing, which was swirling and running my tongue over his prick, and making his dong even harder than it already was.

"Jesus, please tell me this isn't your first time. You are going to become a fine hucow indeed, and when we can finally sell you, we'll make a lot of money."

Even though I shouldn't be feeling this way, I felt overjoyed that they thought I was worth a lot, and more so than most of the hucows in this place.

In the meantime, I just noticed that Stephen didn't feel like being left out. He moved so that he was behind me, pressing his dick against my butt, and then his arms went around me, and his fingers started to pinch and squirt milk out of my udders.

I could feel his mouth near my ear, and I knew he was going to say something to me. "It's just as Jason said, sweetheart. You're finally going to get milked. You are finally going to empty your jugs, and we know how much you want that."

I couldn't say anything. My mouth was filled with Jason's big, meaty dong, and doing anything else that wasn't sucking him off and wetting his prick with my mouth would be like a sin, and I didn't want to do anything wrong, especially after finding out that they were so willing to punish me – including spanking me.

I mumbled something, my tongue running over Jason's prick, and then I started to bob up and down on his length. I didn't know much about what I was doing, just that it was working, and I knew that because he was already moaning and groaning louder than before.

Then, he didn't waste any time, erupting inside of me. His dick started to throb and shake violently, like a beast trapped in its cage. I had to tighten my lips around his dick so that it didn't slip out, and it worked.

And when he was shooting out ropes of his come on my tongue, the salty taste of it graced me with it, and it was a lot more than I thought it was going to be.

I was almost getting overwhelmed, but I didn't say that. What I did was swallow all of his spunk inside my mouth and down my throat as much as I could, and it was everything I could have asked for.

I was still crying, but this time the tears I was shedding were tears of joy, and I couldn't hide that. That was more than evident, and the teachers loved it.

And this time, I knew that they were finally going to penetrate and impale me with their cocks.

CHAPTER 5

It was almost too much for me to take. When he was finally done, he slipped his dick out of my mouth, and I couldn't help but feel that it was a pity it was happening this way. All I wanted right now was his dick back inside my mouth, and it was a shame that he wasn't thinking about doing that.

He shook his dick as if he was teasing me. Seeing that, I couldn't help but look up with pleading eyes. I was hoping that, by doing that, Jason was going to take pity on me, but then I realized that he was smirking. Of course he was going to be smirking. He was always so assured of himself, just like the man that was behind me and whose cock was threatening to go inside of me.

"When I finally take your virginity, you are going to be squirting and cumming all over my cock, and you have no idea how much I want you to do that," he taunted, slipping his dick inside of me, and I was unable to do anything against that.

One moment he was prodding the entrance of my pussy with it, and then the next he was all the way inside of me, but not to the point of popping my hymen yet.

I couldn't help but wonder when he was going to do that, and I was also surprised that Jason didn't say anything about that yet. I thought that they were more territorial. I thought that they were going to be fighting over me, for my attention, to find out who was going to penetrate me first, but it looked like they didn't want to do that, and the thought wasn't even crossing their minds.

Jason was looking now at me with scorn in his eyes. "You can clean it with your tongue, but I suggest you be quick about it. I have a short temper, and I don't like it when I feel like someone is wasting my time."

After he said that, I couldn't help but gulp, and then I noticed that Stephen was already pushing further up against my hymen. Was he really going to do it? Was he really going to pop it? Time was passing and nothing else was happening. He was just teasing me, and I just wanted to punch his face for doing that.

I took a deep breath, running my tongue over Jason's meaty member. I cleaned it up with it and then I looked up with pleading eyes again. I wondered if that was sufficient for him, and it appeared that it was. He was still smirking, and I couldn't be happier for myself.

I did well. I did exactly what he wanted, and now he felt pleased. His smile showed me as much.

"And you think I'm done with you?" He asked, wrapping his finger around his prick and then giving it a couple more strokes, pumping it. Oh my god! Was this really going to happen? Was he really going to orgasm again and shoot his spunk all over me?

I didn't know, but my mind was already thinking about so many things, thoughts swirling in my head, and I couldn't hide my excitement and joy. They showed in my smile, and it went from ear to ear.

"I never thought that," I said and then gasped when I realized that Stephen finally did it. He just popped my hymen, and it was exhilarating, painful, and his cock was so big that he stretched my walls beyond their limits. They would never return to how they were before, and it didn't bother me that it was that way.

I started to cry again, but just like before, this time my tears were tears of joy. Then, he grabbed me tighter, his fingers digging into my skin, and he started to pound against me, in and out of me, fucking me beyond any level I'd thought possible.

In the meantime, I just remembered that Jason was still pumping his prick in front of me, his hand moving faster, and then, no more than a couple of seconds later, he let out a guttural, long groan, and I felt his prick shooting lines of his sperm all over my face, coating me with it, and it was lovely.

My body started to convulse, shake, and I knew I was coming. I was coming another time, and it was happening right when Stephen was also unloading his milk inside of me. He had just gotten me pregnant. I was ovulating, huffing, and sweat was covering my body.

When he was done, it was Jason's turn and I was already getting ready. He took me without showing a hint of mercy, pounding in and out of me, and then he held nothing back, spilling his seed inside of me, and I couldn't help but end all of that with a huge smile on my face.

It couldn't have been any better than it was.

EPILOGUE

The water of the swimming pool felt so nice. I was swimming in it, moving my arms slowly, propelling my body forward until I hit a wall. I pushed myself up, feeling the water moving down on my body, and then I noticed there was a hand in front of my face. It was right in front of my eyes, and after looking further up, I noticed that it was one of my twins' dads that was offering it to me.

He was smiling broadly, and his smile was as bright as the sun. He was shirtless. He wore nothing more than a pair of flimsy shorts, showing off more of his legs than he should.

Checking his legs out, I couldn't help but feel like running my hands on them, feeling the hair, the muscles, the lines, and pretty much everything else that defined them.

And looking at his eyes, I knew he was thinking the same thing. I was pregnant and my belly was growing, so I would have to be careful when doing that.

He pulled me up, helping me until I was sitting on the edge of the swimming pool. Then, he sat down by my side, putting his right arm around my shoulders – it was like he wanted to make sure I remembered that I was his property, and I pretty much was.

Jason liked me so much that he decided to buy me for himself, and I couldn't be any happier about that than I already was. The place where he lived... It was nothing short of stunning, welcoming, and that day when I had first seen it, I knew there was something special about it.

I could feel his arm over my shoulders, on my neck, and I

melted right away.

Leaning in, he said into my ear, "There's a surprise for you, and I hope you're going to like it."

I didn't know what he was talking about, but my heart was already accelerating. I just didn't like waiting for surprises.

And when I was going to ask him what he meant, my ears picked up footsteps coming from behind me. I turned my head around, and then I had to turn my entire body to see the man that was standing in front of me.

He was someone different, which was more surprising than I'd thought. I said that because Jason and Stephen shared everything together, but they were still territorial when it came to me, especially when other men started to ogle me.

I just never thought that they would ever invite anyone over, and much less that it would be such a stunning, hulky man. Muscles on top of muscles, perfect torso, his cock already hard and pressing against his shorts.

I couldn't help but wonder what his name was.

He held out his hand, and I didn't have another choice but to take it. When I did, I realized it was a big mistake that I actually loved. He pulled me to him with force, and then I fell into his arms and he enveloped me in them, keeping me locked tight to him.

He brushed his hand on my cheek, feeling the texture and the softness of the skin. In the meantime, I was feeling the firmness and the roughness of his muscles, and I loved it.

"Something tells me that you were never kissed, Denise," he said, and it surprised me that he knew my name. It meant that Jason and Stephen really trusted him.

To be honest, I wasn't even thinking about it that much. I was trying not to let my body get melted even more than it already was. My knees were like Jell-o, and it was only getting worse, especially when I felt his hand moving down, looking for my ass.

He cupped it, giving it a little squeeze. His lips were so close to mine I thought he was going to kiss me, but he didn't. And just behind his shoulder, I noticed that Stephen was coming this way.

He had a huge smile on his face, and I wondered what he was

going to do when he was right here with us. Was he thinking about fucking me too? I didn't know, but I was hoping that was the case. I knew that I couldn't get pregnant twice, which was a pity, but he could still cum inside of me, and that was all that mattered.

The stranger dipped his head and whispered into my ear what his name was. Mike. It was a beautiful name and it suited him.

He was far from done with me. He wanted more, and he was going to get more. I knew that for certain, especially when he touched his lips to mine, sending shockwaves of pleasure in my body.

If I thought that I could resist my body getting melted even more than it already was, then I had been a fool. The kiss was passionate and hot from the start, and then he held nothing back when slipping his tongue inside my mouth, and I felt like everything was over.

It was all impossible to control.

Then, he pulled his head back, and it was disappointing. I thought that he was going to make the kiss last for all of eternity, but it was obvious that he had other plans in mind, and one of those involved him bending me over, something that he did right away.

My ass was pointed up to the sky, he walked until he was standing behind me, and then he couldn't contain himself, ripping my panties off my body, penetrating me with gusto.

I cried out his name then and there, and when I reopened my eyes, trying to control my breathing, I noticed that two dicks were already positioned in front of my mouth.

I was going to suck them off, it was going to please their owners, and they were going to come out of this looking satisfied.

It was my life's goal to do that.

The End

Looking for more books like this one? Then, check the following pages. There's a teaser for book 1!

Thank you for reading this story. Leave your review. Your feedback helps me immensely!

TEASER: HANDCUFFED FOR BAD BEHAVIOR

Hucow Milking Story - Deimour College 1

Not the place where I wanted to be.

Not with these people looking at me.

I mean, I was in the middle of a crowd, but I was still certain that they were looking at me.

Judging me.

Someone was standing on a raised platform and speaking, but I couldn't pay any attention to his words.

I couldn't stop thinking that something had to be wrong with this. All the hucows were women and all the trainers and professors were men.

Obviously, all the hucows were going to be women, but all the teachers were men? What the hell was going on here?

They were keeping us naked in the main hall, and we couldn't do anything about it.

One peep and it would be enough to put us in their cells.

They were cold, unforgiving. I couldn't stand even thinking about those cells, and I was certain that it would never happen to me.

The teachers would never put us in one of those cells.

It didn't matter that they were all smoking hot.

They were never going to make me think that anything could ever happen between us.

Even though...

Even though the reason why I came here was simple.

I thought that I could strike gold by coming here. Thought that one of the teachers would have eyes for me, but that lasted until I realized that they were all married.

And I wasn't lying. All of them had marriage rings on their fingers, destroying all hope that I once had. So why did I even think that coming here was going to solve anything?

The truth was that it wasn't going to solve anything.

We were all here, in the main hall, and the teacher on the raised platform was speaking about what our lives here were going to be like.

It was like time was passing but wasn't at the same time.

I took a deep breath in, closed my eyes, and thought that for sure nothing else was going to happen here.

We were going to be taken to our bedrooms, they were going to lock us in there, and that was going to be it.

I was so certain of that that I wasn't even aware of what was happening around me or what my ears were hearing.

That was why I was so stunned when I noticed someone right by my side, and it wasn't one of the candidates.

It was actually a man. One of the teachers, I noticed right away. He was nothing short of stunning.

He looked just like all the other teachers, but he was also different.

Blond hair.

Stubble on his face.

Square jawline.

Full lips.

A massive, hulky body.

And eyes that looked into mine as though he could read everything I was thinking.

Even though I wasn't even trying to say anything, I felt like I was mumbling. I was so stunned that my body had frozen up. And I was certain that he was aware of the effect he was having on me. It was why he wasn't smiling right now.

Such a devilish, evil smile, and he wasn't ashamed of it.

And I was certain that he knew how aroused he was making me feel, too.

After all, why else would he be pulling up the side of his lips like that, showing me a little of his teeth? Even though I couldn't see much, there was no denying that they were shining.

"Who are you?" I asked, hoping that he was going to be forthcoming with his answer, but knowing that he didn't have to.

He didn't say anything for the first few seconds, making me feel so anxious, and I was certain he was using that to his advantage as well.

If there was something I learned about the teachers here in Deimour College, it was that they had no boundaries when it came to taking advantage of their students.

"I'm Jason. I'm one of the teachers here in the college," he replied, not giving me any new information. Of course he wouldn't.

"I already knew that," I said, my eyes moving up and down while I felt some wetness and heat between my legs. It was impossible not to be feeling that way when he was so hot and was so incredibly close to me.

He was so close that he was making it difficult for me to breathe.

I just couldn't stop scrutinizing every part of his body.

His rippling muscles.

His bulging biceps.

His crotch.

The way his shirt showed off his abs.

And pretty much everything else. The more I looked at this man, Jason, the more I felt absolutely stunned.

And that made me feel like doing something I thought I never would.

Bad behavior.

Behaving in a way that would put me into trouble.

I knew that was a mistake, but I was still willing to go through with it until the end.

But what would be my punishment if that happened?

"Do you want something from me?" I asked and for the time being, it was like everything happening around me didn't matter anymore.

"I don't know. You tell me."

I checked him out from bottom to top again, my eyes lingering on his crotch. I didn't know if he was wearing tight boxer briefs, but his bulge was so big, and it kept on making me think about what it would be like to feel it with my fingers.

Should I do that? I didn't know, and I was soon realizing that I had to make a decision. After all, the other teacher, whose name I didn't know, was already moving away from the raised platform after speaking his lines in front of the students.

We were all going somewhere else, but I realized that I didn't have to.

After all, Jason was with me.

His eyes were staring at me.

"I think you know what I want from you, and I think you also know why you came here."

He was so sure of himself that it was maddening, and it still melted my heart.

Could I really not do what he wanted? The more time passed here, the more I realized that it was impossible not to.

Thus, without giving it a second thought, I just moved away with him somewhere else.

But we weren't going with the other teachers and the students. We were going to a separate room in Deimour College, and I couldn't wait for some sexy time with Jason.

I knew he was unbelievably hung.

SIMILAR BOOKS

BUNDLE - HUCOW PRISON

All the books of the Hucow Prison series in one single, convenient collection.

1. Hucow Prison

SERIES - FERTILE ONLY

1. Bumping the Teacher

2. Bumping the Midwife

3. Bumping the Farmhand

4. Bumping the Sinner

SERIES - HIS HERD

1. Peculiar Dairy

2. Milked by her Boyfriend

3. Menage for Milking

4. Farm Milking

5. Fertile for my Farmers

ABOUT THE AUTHOR

Leandra Camilli's obsession? Writing dirty, steamy stories that make her readers drool. She loves her Alpha males, hucows, sissies, and futas. If you're looking for those kinds of books, look no further.

With a cup of coffee on her table and warm socks on, she writes almost every day. Leandra Camilli has featured in several top 100 categories in the store, and she publishes weekly.